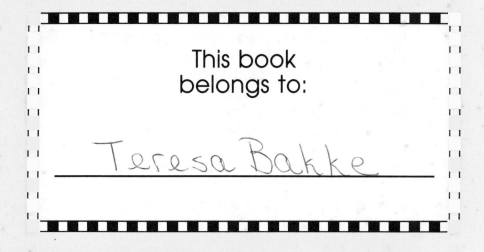

This book
belongs to:

Teresa Bakke

MESSAGE TO PARENTS

This book is perfect for parents and children to read aloud together. First read the story to your child. When you read it again run your finger under each line, stopping at each picture for your child to "read." Help your child to figure out the picture. If your child makes a mistake, be encouraging as you say the right word. Point out the written word beneath each picture in the margin on the page. Soon your child will be "reading" aloud with you, and at the same time learning the symbols that stand for words.

EDITED BY
DEBORAH SHINE

DESIGN BY
CANARD DESIGN, INC.

Elsie's Clean Day

A Read Along With Me Book

By Debby Slier

Illustrated by Kitty Diamantis

CHECKERBOARD PRESS
NEW YORK

Elsie

bath

eyes

ears

 had just had a . She

hated having a . The water

got into her and , and

she didn't like the taste of

soap.

When she was dry,  looked

in the  .

"How clean I am," she thought.

"And that's the way I am going

to stay. No more s for me!"

mirror

Elsie

Mother

cookie

tail

hands

 walked into the kitchen.

 was baking s .

wagged her . "Look how

clean I am!" smiled and

offered a .

wanted the , but she saw

the flour on 's .

"No way I'm going to get flour on me!" said  . "No more s for me!"  walked out the  and into the yard.

 was working on the car. "Hi,  ," he called. But  saw the grease on his  and walked right past him and the  . "No grease on me, and no more s!" she said to herself.

bath

door

Father

car

Elsie

Jan

box

bath

Next saw in the sand . Digging in the sand with was one of 's favorite games. Today she walked right past .

"No digging in the sand for me, and no more s!"

Grandma

Grandpa

tree

 and were in the garden. They were busy planting some little s.

"Too much dirt there," said , and she lay down in the shade of the old willow . "No more 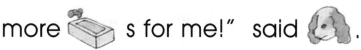s for me!" said . "I am going to stay clean."

Elsie

birds

birdbath

bath

cat

 lay with her head on her

front paws. She watched the

playing in the . "No s

for me," said . "I'm not a

bird." Max the came into

the garden. All the flew

away. "Max never has a ," said 🐕. "🐈s are lucky."

She saw the 🐕 from next door playing under the 🪢 with his friends.

Just then 👧 called . "Come on, 🐕 , let's play with them!"

But 🐕 didn't answer. She just lay and watched her friends having fun.

dog

hose

Jan

bath

Elsie

Jan

ball

eyes

"I'm not going anywhere that will get me dirty. I'm not having any more s!" lay still and watched play with their friends.

 began to feel lonely. She closed her . She thought of the fun she had when

threw a  for her to fetch.

She thought about the times

when they splashed through the

rain together.

🐕 heard the 🔵 bounce.

She opened her 🐶 . The 🔵

was right in front of her 👃 .

stick

nose

ball

Jan

Elsie

hose

She picked up the and

carried it to her friends.

threw the again.

couldn't resist running after it. This

time it landed under the .

 ran after the .

Muddy water splashed onto her

beautiful clean coat.

"I'm only a little dirty," she said

to herself.  threw the

again, and before long

forgot all about being clean.

She had mud splattered all over

her coat.  was dirty again!

She knew she would have to

have ANOTHER .

bath

 gave a happy bark. She remembered how good 's s, fresh out of the oven, tasted. She remembered how nice it felt to have  stroke her. She also remembered the nice warm feeling she got when

 or  talked gently to her

and scratched behind her .

But most of all she remembered

that playing with friends was the

best feeling of all... even though

she got dirty and had to have

another  ...it was worth it.

Grandma

Grandpa

ears

bath

Elsie

bath

 barked happily as she thought, "Having a isn't so bad... especially when getting dirty is so much fun."

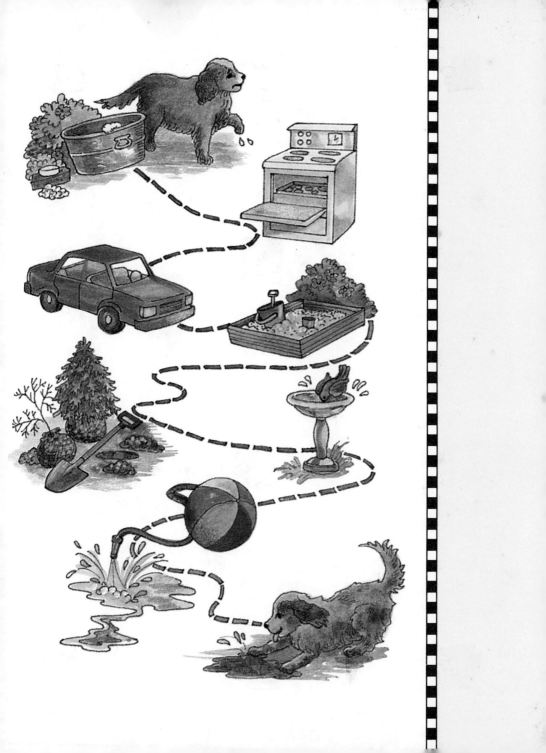